The Page we refuse to Turn

The Page We Refuse to Turn

Turn the Page

Bishop A W Sease

XULON PRESS

Xulon Press
2301 Lucien Way #415
Maitland, FL 32751
407.339.4217
www.xulonpress.com

© 2022 by Bishop A W Sease

Contribution by: Karen Bazemore

All rights reserved solely by the author. The author guarantees all contents are original and do not infringe upon the legal rights of any other person or work. No part of this book may be reproduced in any form without the permission of the author.

Due to the changing nature of the Internet, if there are any web addresses, links, or URLs included in this manuscript, these may have been altered and may no longer be accessible. The views and opinions shared in this book belong solely to the author and do not necessarily reflect those of the publisher. The publisher therefore disclaims responsibility for the views or opinions expressed within the work.

Unless otherwise indicated, Scripture quotations taken from The Message (MSG). Copyright © 1993, 1994, 1995, 1996, 2000, 2001, 2002. Used by permission of NavPress Publishing Group. Used by permission. All rights reserved.

Scripture quotations taken from the Holy Bible, New International Version (NIV). Copyright © 1973, 1978, 1984, 2011 by Biblica, Inc.™. Used by permission. All rights reserved.

Scripture quotations taken from the King James Version (KJV)–*public domain.*

Paperback ISBN-13: 978-1-66286-483-4
Ebook ISBN-13: 978-1-66286-484-1

Contents

Endorsement by Bishop Lloyd T. Alston........................ix
Endorsement by Pastor Victor Correa xi
Endorsement by Pastor Cherring A. Spence xiii
Endorsement by Pastor Jeffrey Goodson xv
Endorsement by First Lady Patricia Sease xvii
Introduction xix
My Inspiration: Story from the Beach........................xxi
Chapter 1: I Was Stuck and Did Not Know It 1
    Depletion: Where Is Your Hope?.........................3
Chapter 2: Reaching Beyond 7
    Forgiveness..8
    Let Go and Let God....................................10
    Reaching In...11
Chapter 3: Fear of the Unknown 15
    Global Pandemics 16
    Messed-Up People......................................18
Chapter 4: What Happens When We Defy Nature? 23
    Development, Not Punishment...........................25
Chapter 5: Dare to Be Different 29
    Gatekeepers...32
Chapter 6: No Manufacturer's Recall...........................35
    Deeper Walk or Plow Pusher?...........................38
Chapter 7: Transformation 41
Notes 47

Endorsement by Bishop Lloyd T. Alston

**Presiding Bishop, Covenant Kingdom Fellowship Assembly
Lead Pastor, Cornerstone Covenant Church
Roanoke Rapids, North Carolina**

Proverbs 14:12–13 from the New Revised Standard Version declares, *"There is a way that seems right to a person, but its end is the way to death. Even in laughter the heart is sad, and the end of joy is grief."* In *The Page We Refuse to Turn,* Bishop Anthony W. Sease peels the layers of the onion all the way to its core all while providing a path to the "more excellent way" (**1 Cor. 12:31**). This text is not just a quick read, but it is a qualitative reference and handbook to help someone to muster up the strength to just turn the page and take the first step toward the new way of life. After reading this book, you will agree that we don't have to stay in the shape that we're in. There is hope, and there is help!

Endorsement by Pastor Victor Correa

**Associate Pastor of Administration
Director of Word Alive Study
New Covenant Community Church
York, Pennsylvania**

Bishop Sease's first book *The Page We Refuse to Turn* provides passionate pastoral advice on how and why we need to turn the negative page(s) of our lives to experience a victorious and successful fulfilling life!

It is a book you can devour now. Get ready!

Endorsement by Pastor Cherring A. Spence

Overseeing Pastor
The Gathering Well, Inc.
Baltimore, Maryland

Applause for *The Page We Refuse to Turn!*

Many are held prisoner by the past. Sometimes the past seems inescapable. This book empowers those readers who grasp the book's message to let go of the past and walk triumphantly into the future.

The following scriptures flooded my mind as I considered endorsing this book: *"And the LORD answered me, and said, Write the vision, and make it plain upon tables, that he may run that readeth it. For the vision is yet for an appointed time, but at the end it shall speak and not lie: though it tarry, wait for it; because it will surely come, it will not tarry . . . O LORD, revive thy work in the midst of the years."* **(Hab. 2:2–3; 3:2b, KJV)**

Thank you for the honor and the privilege of being among one of the first to read your book. Congratulations on writing such a timely and thought-provoking work. Thank you for penning this vision and laying it out on the pages of your compelling book plainly upon the table. Your book is a crucial tool God will use to "revive the work in the midst of the years" for individuals, servant leaders, and churches at large. I pray for remarkable success.

Endorsement by Pastor Jeffrey Goodson

District Superintendent COGIC
Pastor of Chose Generation
Philadelphia, Pennsylvania

It is during these days of uncertainty and disappointment that we are introduced to a read that's both inspiring and has content with a mesmerizing message. Kudos to Bishop Anthony Sease for recognizing the heartbeat of the body of Christ and presenting us with such empowerment. Let's turn the page.

Endorsement by First Lady Patricia Sease

**Associate Pastor of Women's Ministry
New Covenant Community Church
York, Pennsylvania**

To Bishop Anthony W. Sease, my husband, as I read this book which you have penned, *The Page We Refuse to Turn*, it took me back a few years to that day in the State of Virginia while on vacation. It was a very hot day at the beach, and as we relaxed in our lounge chairs, there was a person who walked along the beach dressed in an overcoat, hat, and scarf. He looked at us, we looked back at him, and you could see on his face that he was content. He did not feel as if he was over-dressed for the hot weather. His glare at my husband and me was as if we were under-dressed for the warm weather.

My husband immediately said to me, "What am I supposed to see out of this?" He pondered that thought for a while, then said to me that evening, "Some people are really stuck on a page. I'm going to title my book *The Page We Refuse to Turn*."

It's been about six years ago now, and to finally see the book come to fruition is a great accomplishment. I truly believe this book will help move the reader forward if we just follow God's instructions to move from the past and turn the page.

I am godly proud of you for completing this project.

Introduction

Written to encourage the readers to allow the Holy Spirit to examine their hearts, *The Page We Refuse to Turn* is designed to help the body of Christ wake up and walk in wholeness for such a time as this **(Esther 4:14)**. Each chapter will challenge you to look beyond your traditions and brokenness so you can transform into a new way of life. You will no longer stay stuck in your unsuccessfulness or duplicate an ineffective prayer life. Neglecting to take your place in the kingdom of God as joint heirs with Christ and to be glorified with Him **(Rom. 8:17)** is to neglect the very core of your being and deny why you were created. According to dictionary.com, the word *refuse* means to decline to accept; reject.

Beloved, please accept Jesus as your Lord and Savior today so you can walk in freedom. May the time you spend studying this book help you to willingly submit yourself to the Potter who desires to reshape your life. Our world is changing all around us, with wars and rumors of wars, pandemics, socialism, extreme poverty, and refugees from many countries fleeing for their lives; therefore, we must look to our Creator for the answers.

Get ready, get ready, get ready!

My Inspiration: Story from the Beach

Recently during a family vacation at Virginia Beach, I occupied my favorite relaxed position on my beach chair that included an adjustable pillow, storage pouches, and a folding towel bar with an umbrella rental to keep me comfortable as I soaked up the sun's rays. Meanwhile, my lovely wife, First Lady Trish, was doing her typical shoreline walk as her feet were covered by the gentle waves of the Atlantic Ocean. As I quietly sat enjoying the atmosphere with the laughter of children playing, water splashing, and teens participating in a volleyball game, my eyes were drawn to an individual who was dressed as if it were zero degrees outside. Trust me when I say it was close to 100 degrees with plenty of humidity, but that did not seem to move this person. In fact, the closer this person came to me, the more I realized how comfortable the individual was and how convinced the person was that those of us in bathing suits, swim shorts, and t shirts were completely crazy!

I could not shake this image. I believe the Holy Spirit was showing me how the body of Christ should be in the world, but not of it **(John 17:14–15)**. We should not have the same value system, which requires us to be free of worldly influence. It means that we should not act as the unsaved world does; therefore, we should look and operate differently.

> We are not slaves to our sinful natures, but ought to act in accordance with righteousness **(Rom. 6:6, 11)**.

We are told to put to death things that are of our sinful natures and to flee from immorality **(Col. 3:5–10; 1 Cor. 6:18; Gal. 5:16–24; Eph. 5:3–11)**.

We train ourselves for godliness **(1 Tim. 4:7)** and are imitators of God **(Eph. 5:1)**.

We should be preparing ourselves for good works to meet the needs of the poor and build up the kingdom of God **(Titus 3:1)**.

"We are ambassadors for Christ" **(2 Cor. 5:20)**, spreading His fragrance **(2 Cor. 2:15–16)** through the world.

In essence, we act according to the new nature we have been given rather than the sinful nature of our flesh **(2 Cor. 5:17, 21; Titus 3:3–8)**.

Do you have the audacity to be different or are you trying to just fit in?

According to **1 Peter 2:9**, we are *"a chosen race, a royal priesthood, a holy nation, a people for his own possession, that you may proclaim the excellencies of him who called you out of darkness into his marvelous light."* We live in a fallen world, but we should not act like those who do not know Christ. We are to be the light since we know Christ. And while we are still in the world, we are *"called to be set apart, to shine the light that others might know Him and be saved"* **(Matt. 5:13–16)**.

Beloved, are you *really* being the light and leading others to Christ, or has the church dozed off and allowed itself to be lulled, hushed, and soothed into a disinclined slumber? Like most people, I am a visual learner. The Lord used the image of light as an aid to keep the message imprinted on my brain to inspire and compel me to share the dire significance and meaning for His people everywhere. Let us explore and investigate within the following pages how we can arouse, reconnect, and reengage in righteousness.

Gear up, saints! The victory is ours to take!

Chapter 1:

I Was Stuck and Did Not Know It

Suffice to say that many people, including the church, the body of Christ, are unknowingly caught in a time warp instead of declaring that, like Jesus, *"I come in the volume of the book that is written of me, to do His will"* **(Heb. 10:7)**. Sure, there are many reasons for this lack of movement, like brokenness, traditions, poverty, nutritional deficiencies, educational disparities, denominational discrepancies, or the breakdown of the family structure to name a few. This absence of motivation represents pages or seasons of our lives that we refuse to turn **(John 17:14–15)**.

For example, if a child suffered some sort of pain that caused trauma like physical abuse, bullying, or body shaming and never processed it through counseling, deliverance, prayer, and parental intervention, then they could potentially stop themselves from attending college to avoid confrontation. Similarly, if an adolescent or young adult has been sexually abused, has an eating disorder, or a learning disability, they may never try to look beyond their limitations to live up to their God-given potential.

Others may allow financial shortages, cultural customs, or negative and/or false labels to keep them stuck in a rut. These same people feel silenced and push their emotions down deep, but grow into parched adulthood. They train themselves to survive and, unfortunately, never learn to thrive. They are thirsty and yearn for validation. They attract others who are trapped in the same dysfunctional cycles, familiar spirits, and bondages **(1 Chron. 10:13–14)** while they struggle to hold down a job to provide for their children. Despite their best efforts, the pain they carry inside further isolates them from godly contentment. As wounded adults, they carry this defective mentality into the church. Various offices that include ushers, choir members, ministers, teachers, pastors, and bishops in the Lord are filled with people in bondage to their past. This existence has become a way of life.

They are stuck and, in many cases, don't even know it.

Some refuse to turn a page in their lives because it's all they know, and it has become uncomfortably comfortable for them. They are familiar with the mediocre routines and no longer desire to rock the boat to do anything more. In their hearts, they want more but settle for putting their ambitions for better tucked away on a hidden shelf. It's a nice idea when others remind them of their possibilities, but they keep it as a distant pipedream. They are never quite cozy in this state of mind, but reject a healthier lifestyle. Despite their spiritual development, they are okay with it. They know better, but they refuse to do better.

Our brokenness affects the way we perceive things, like a polarizing filter on a camera that saturates colors and reduces reflections, but hinders our ability to understand the complete picture. We incorrectly interpret life through our pain. It cripples us personally and spiritually, which hinders our relationship with our families, co-workers, and, ultimately, our heavenly Father. As a result, this same brokenness weakens and adversely effects the body of Christ corporately. As the saying goes, "a chain is only as strong as its weakest link," which means that the church is only as strong or successful as its unproductive or fruitless member(s). We need to take back our lives and our families.

How does a single, broken parent try to love and train their children up in the Lord **(Prov. 22:6)**? They are not alone but are not sure how to push past their pain. They can only teach what they know. Even with two broken parents, how do they model unconditional love when they were violated, abused, or abandoned as children? What about all of the children who grow up in foster care through no fault of their own due to their having been neglected by their drug-addicted parents? How do they teach a new generation about a loving Savior/Provider/Healer?

We need to learn how to be delivered and break free from unproductive cycles and strongholds to avoid duplicating repetitive customs and quoting wearisome prayers that lead to emptiness and unsuccessfulness. We will further explore how we can *all* connect to a loving God who will never leave us or forsake us and who wants to deliver us from our pasts, strongholds, and demonic bondages that seek to keep us bound. As individuals and/or parents, we *do not* have to stay broken; instead, we can learn how to walk in liberty with the Lover of our souls and teach our children and others how to choose the road to freedom.

Depletion: Where Is Your Hope?

Far too many are afflicted and tormented physically and emotionally as they are bleeding out with no relief in sight. Additionally, they are thirsty as they aimlessly wander through dry seasons in their lives. Some are desperate after spending thousands of dollars on doctors and specialists to no avail. Others mask their pain in substance and alcohol addiction for temporary or momentary reprieve. Where is your expectation?

I am reminded of **Mark 5:24–34** when a woman who had been subject to bleeding for twelve years suffered a great deal under the care of many doctors. She spent all she had, yet instead of getting better, she grew worse. Verses 27 through 29 tell us, *"when she heard about Jesus, she came up behind him in the crowd and touched his cloak, because she thought, 'If I just touch the hem of His garment, I will be healed.' Immediately her bleeding stopped, and she felt in her body that she was freed from her suffering."* Don't miss her activity as the Bible makes it clear that she endured for many years and sought help from experts. She heard about a loving Savior, a Provider, and, yes, a Healer. The Bible *does not* identify who told her, but when she heard the good news of this Savior and the signs and wonders that followed Him, she believed—so much so that she purposed in her heart to act.

Touching the "hem" means fringe, tassel, or the border of a garment. **Numbers 15:38–39** states, *"Speak to the children of Israel: Tell them to make tassels on the corners of their garments throughout their generations, and to put a blue thread in the tassels of the corners. And you shall have the tassel, that you may look upon it and remember all the commandments of the LORD and do them."* She took a big risk to press her way through the crowd, since she was bleeding and considered unclean, meaning everything she touched was considered unclean. I can imagine she tried to stay low and covered so no one would notice or recognize her. She had a determination in her heart that she no longer wanted to be stuck in her circumstances. She wanted to turn the page of her book, so she sought out deliverance. She touched an intimate part of His garment that is a reminder to the wearer to keep and do the commandments of the Lord, so she wanted to join her faith with His divine power.

Verse 30 tells us that Jesus realized at once that power had gone out from Him. He turned around in the crowd and asked, "Who touched me?" Beloved, Jesus felt the impact of her faith and knew someone was set free! Hallelujah! Verse 31 tells us that His disciples were oblivious to what just happened and responded in the natural way instead of in the spirit. *"You see the people crowding against you, and yet you can ask, 'Who touched me?'"* Regardless of their inexperience, Jesus kept looking around to see who had done it. The fact that it was not easy for Jesus and His disciples to promptly identify this woman is a testament of her lowliness and ability to blend into the crowd undetectably. The story ends with her risking exposure but responding to the Savior's question in verses 33 and 34: *"Then the woman, knowing what had happened to her, came and fell at his feet and, trembling with fear, told him the whole truth. He said to her, 'Daughter, your faith has healed you. Go in peace and be freed from your suffering.'"*

Beloved, don't stay stuck—turn the page!

Get into an intimate place with the Lord, and let Him heal you. Start by praying and accepting Jesus as your Lord today, right now! Time is not promised to you, neither is your next breath. Believe in your heart that He died on the cross for *you* and ask Him to forgive you of every sin you have ever committed **(Rom. 10:9–10)**. Ask Jesus to come into your heart to be your Lord and Savior, then thank Him for placing your name in the Book of Life **(Rev. 3:5)**.

Next, ask Jesus to heal every part of your heart that hurts. Let Him fill you with His unconditional love and joy in exchange for your pain and sadness. Let Him bestow upon you a crown of glory instead of ashes, the oil of gladness instead of mourning, and a garment of praise instead of a spirit of despair **(Isa. 61:1)**. Give it to Him. Stop carrying around the weight of your sorrow, and *don't* pick it back up.

Chapter 2:

Reaching Beyond

How do we stretch beyond our break ups, break downs, and break outs? How do we keep it together when everyone and everything around us seems to be out of our control? How do you hold on when you want to let go? Where do we go for stability and strength?

Social media and cable news programs shows images of people of all racial backgrounds fighting just to stay alive. Sending our children to school has even become a gamble at best, for teachers are getting locked up for inappropriate relationships with minors, bullying is out of control (even driving some students to suicide), and armed individuals with mental health problems are invading the buildings to gun down children. It happens in the cities and suburbs alike in many states. Innocent blood is being shed everywhere. Some people are so lost and immaturely stuck that the only option they see is to formulate a plot to cause harm to the young.

The struggle is real.

Where do we turn to when history shows us that our justice system does not always practice equality in diverse communities? Clearly varied children, men, and women of color—including Asians, African Americans, Pacific Islanders, Puerto Ricans, American Indians, and Mexicans—are not always treated with dignity and respect. We cannot keep looking the other way and think it will somehow go away. On the contrary, it has gotten worse. These people are stuck in reverse. Not only have they refused to turn a page, but they went backwards and don't know how to move forward. Sure, they have been taught this concept and saw it demonstrated by their parents and grandparents, but where does it end? Every effort to bring unity and impartiality matters, and a single step in the right direction can make a huge difference. How do we bridge the gap between cultural clashes and those in authority?

We start right where we are, for each person is at a different place. Please be aware that God never fails to notice anyone, including the individuals our vain society would rather not acknowledge. Our heavenly Father took a big step to show each and every one of us how much He loves us. *"For God so loved the world that He gave . . ."* (**John 3:16**). What did He so willingly give? His only Son, Jesus Christ, *"that whosoever believes in Him shall not perish but have eternal life!"*

Have you accepted Jesus as your Lord and Savior? Jesus bore *all* of our sins on the cross so we don't have to live in shame and sorrow or despair and depression. God made Him who knew no sin to be sin on our behalf so that in Him we might become the righteousness of God (**2 Cor. 5:21**). We are *all* here for a reason, and our lives matter. Nobody is a mistake.

Beloved, *you* are dearly loved (**Col. 3:12**). You are the apple of His eye (**Ps. 17:8; Prov. 7:2**). Yes, *you!*

Forgiveness

The negative behaviors we are witnessing today are not God's best for anyone. Just like God can forgive us for all of our sins, we must also forgive others (**Eph. 4:32**). What do you do with parents who fell short due to drugs, alcohol, or selfish ambitions? Forgive them. How do you bounce back when you love someone who does not love you back? Forgive them. Even if your best friend snuck behind your back and stole your boyfriend or girlfriend, what do you do? Forgive them. What about the perpetrator who accidently killed your innocent grandchild who was sitting on the front porch because of a drive-by shooting incident even though she was never the target? Forgive them.

Forgiveness does not mean we become doormats; it means we do not allow someone else's sin to poison our hearts and manifest itself as a root of bitterness inside of us. It can start out as anger and resentment, then grow into something that dominates, manipulates, and ultimately controls us. Forgiveness sets *us* free, not the perpetrator(s). They may or may not keep going and repeating negative behaviors in other states; you may never even see them again. Whatever the case, hopefully they accept Jesus as their Lord and Savior. Forgiving them means you are not trapped by their sin, bad dreams, or memories; instead, the Lord wants to take the pain away and help you learn from it so it no longer controls your emotions when you may be reminded about it or prevent you from becoming obsessed with it.

Since we know that we are born in sin **(Rom. 5:12)**, let me propose a rhetorical question. How many sins have you committed over the years? Perhaps way too many to count. I submit to you that forgiveness is a way of life.

Our flawed justice system evaluates the degree of infractions or violations of the law and assigns consequences based on preset regulations and penalties. **First John 5:17** states that *all* unrighteousness is sin. We cannot pick and choose who we forgive nor is it exclusive to certain sins; it goes across the board. As a believer, the Lord forgave us of our sins. Not just some, but *all*. Yes, it can be difficult to start the process when you don't "feel" like forgiving them; however, you can ask the Lord to help you to forgive so you can walk in freedom. You may have to continuously pray day after day, week after week, and month after month before you feel the release. Yet the healing of your wounds is worth it!

Beloved, turn the page of the volume of the book that is written for you. Refusing to turn the page *does not* help you in any way. In fact, it keeps you locked in your own prison. As a result, you teach these neurotic behaviors and strongholds to your children, neighbors, and anyone who will listen, placing them deeper into the same prison.

Let Go and Let God

Stop pointing fingers and blaming others. Yes, I know you have been hurt, but you can choose to walk in love. I am not minimalizing your trauma or pain; I am merely suggesting that you take back your life. Don't let the enemy rob you of your youth or potential to be all that you can be in Christ as an adult. Allow Christ to envelope you in His strong arms and cause you to experience a tidal wave of hope and love. **Psalm 34:18** tells us that the Lord is close to the brokenhearted and saves those who are crushed in spirit. He is always close to the lost and lonely. Additionally, **Matthew 12:20** describes how much Christ wants to help you walk in freedom, *"a bruised reed he will not break, and a smoldering wick he will not snuff out, till He has brought justice through to victory."* God is our refuge and strength, an ever-present help in trouble **(Ps. 46:1)**. Beloved, hold on. He is not finished writing your story. Turning a page can require courage and depth, so give it to the Lord and let Him transform your life.

Next, let go of the past, the pain, and the person(s) who transgressed against you and lose yourself in the Holy Spirit! That's right, begin to worship the Lord. Raise your hands and lift your voice. You can start by thanking Him for life, forgiveness, freedom, and sending His Son to die on the cross for your sins **(John 3:16)**. Ask Him to help you to receive and understand His unconditional love for you so you can show that love to everyone around you.

Third, you must shift your thinking and realize your role as the bride of Jesus. Men might struggle with that since they are used to being the groom, but Jesus is coming back for His bride (the body of Christ). Make His priorities your priorities. His heart of compassion should be your heart of compassion. What moves Him should move you. *"For in Him we live, and move, and have our being"* **(Acts 17:28)**. Beloved, we must have a committed and personal relationship with Jesus Christ. To know Him is to receive His love. The lover of your soul will give you the strength to turn the page(s) of your life.

Reaching In

In order to progress in our lives, we need to make some type of movement—preferably forward, maybe even sometimes sideways. What we don't want to do is move backwards or mark time by standing still. It takes different things to motivate different people. In **Philippians 3:3-14**, Paul uses the analogy of a runner who focuses on the goal ahead of him. Learn to set goals, saints. Make one of them to model the behavior and teach someone else like your families and neighbors. This prevents doubts and distractions.

Paul's spiritual goal is stated directly in verse 14, *"the prize of the upward call of God in Christ Jesus."* What are your goals? Make them specific. Verse 13 makes it clear that Paul's focus is on forward momentum, not his past that may include failures or pain. How can you move ahead or turn the page if you are stuck in your past? You cannot. Paul was focused on going to heaven and did not let anything sidetrack him.

Churches should be a place to help you grow spiritually to support your efforts to stay focused. Spiritual education should equip families with God's truth as defined in the B.I.B.L.E.—Bodily Instructions Before Leaving Earth—to be used as a fortified defense against a culture that opposes God. The Lord said His people are destroyed because of lack of knowledge **(Hos. 4:6)**, so we know that information and wisdom is essential. Godly instructions that edify the mind, body, and spirit are key to understanding who we are in Christ. You must be conscientious in choosing the right place to fellowship so you understand your worth. You have been purchased with a price **(1 Cor. 2:20)**. Exposure to God's truth is fundamental to obtain holy boldness. We need to learn to glorify God with our hearts, thoughts, entertainment, and lifestyle choices. He bought us back from the grips of the enemy with the shedding of His blood.

You have free will so you can do what you want. We all must come to a point in our lives where we decide whether we will serve Him or not. Are you willing to consecrate yourself, which means to be separate and set apart? Your worth and value is not in your job, paycheck, house, car, or title. Are you willing to take the time, expend the effort, and take the risks to be devoted to God despite what culture thinks, says, or does? Your responses have everything to do with your willingness, or lack of, to bend, twist, or turn your page so you can walk in freedom.

Eugene Peterson in *A Long Obedience in the Same Direction* wrote:

> *"It is not difficult in our world to get a person interested in the message of the Gospel; it is terrifically difficult to sustain the interest. Millions of people in our culture make decisions for Christ, but there is a dreadful attrition rate. Many claim to have been born again, but the **evidence for mature Christian discipleship is slim**. There is a great market for religious experience in our world; there is little enthusiasm for the patient acquisition of virtue, little inclination to sign up for a long apprenticeship in what earlier Christians called holiness. The Christian life is not a hundred-yard dash; **it's a marathon, a long obedience in the same direction.**"* (Peterson, 2000)

This may shake a lot of people who are undercover Christians—never making their spirituality known to those around them since they are more influenced by society's standards. Christian values rarely line up with humanity and popular culture; therefore, choices must be made accordingly. Stay anchored in your faith in the Lord for the long haul, not a quick fix. It's okay to call on Him during a crisis, but after His response, we make it clear that we can handle the rest until another situation happens. Some people stay in crisis mode. Disciples are made in the deep waters, not in the shallow end. **Luke 5:5 (NLT)** states why we should simply obey God in the deep waters of life: *"'Master,' Simon replied, 'we worked hard all last night and didn't catch a thing. **But if you*

***say so**, I'll let the nets down again.'"* When the disciples obeyed Jesus, they needed extra help to pull up all of the fish.

Just submit and act when He speaks and watch your life change. If He tells you to love, to go, to give, to serve—do it. The battleground starts in the mind and your will. Give God a full *yes!* Step out and trust Him. In your obedience, the Holy Spirit will give you the courage you need to turn the page.

Chapter 3:

Fear of the Unknown

The results of your inability to switch pages greatly affects everything you express to the people around you. In order to overcome your strongholds that affect your seasons, you must acknowledge them and learn to silence the lies and the F.E.A.R.—Fake Evidence Appearing Real. Many of us believe false propaganda that says you are not good enough or you are ugly or nobody loves you. We fear rejection, loss of health, death, job security, ability to pay bills, marriage, divorce, food/housing uncertainties, and more in an attempt to achieve some type of security. Remember, these are all fabrications from the enemy designed to keep you trapped.

When your reaction is stronger than the incident, then we know that there is a deceptive history attached. Think about it: if you are bothered every time you see a little girl holding her father's hand walking down the street and you holler at him to leave her alone, you think you are saving the child because your father used to take you by the hand and lead you into your bedroom to molest you. Truly, you are bound by the past and have not turned that page. You don't have to fear your past or problems.

Beloved, you are more than a conqueror in Christ Jesus (**Rom. 8:37**). You have everything you need from the Lord to be an awesome man or woman of God in your spirit. **Ephesians 4:30** states we are marked and branded by God. When you believe or think differently, you will act differently. **Romans 8:12–16** encourages believers to live in agreement with the Bible.

> *Therefore, brothers and sisters, we have an obligation—but it is not to the flesh, to live according to it. For if you live according to the flesh, you will die; but if by the Spirit you put to death the misdeeds of the body, you will live. For those who are led by the Spirit of God are the children of God. The Spirit you received does not make you slaves, so that you live in **fear again**; rather, the Spirit you received brought about your adoption to sonship. And by him we cry, 'Abba, Father.' The Spirit himself testifies with our spirit that we are God's children.*

There is no fear in love; perfect love casts out fear **(1 John 4:18)**. As His children, we are empowered to walk in His love; then there is no room for false evidence appearing real. Jesus is our security.

Global Pandemics

Despite knowing Christ, some of us still walk in fear, so I believe God permits interruptions to force us to evaluate our priorities. If we continue to refuse to turn the page, He will allow things that ultimately shake things up to turn the page for us! Take, for instance, the COVID-19 virus that spread worldwide in 2020; certainly, it did not take the Lord by surprise. In fact, it is not the first pandemic humanity has encountered—the Spanish flu (H1N1 influenza) of 1918 was very similar. Both caused global pandemics that targeted everyone regardless of age, economic status, or ethnic background, and both were highly infectious, spreading through respiratory droplets. People were forced to wear masks to protect themselves from contracting the viruses (Gillespie, p. 1).

Businesses and schools closed. Quarantines were enforced. Who would have guessed in this day and age that our world would come to a screeching halt? The national and local news stations were reporting how our economy plummeted, our hospitals were so inundated with those infected with the virus that other critical patients could not be treated, and makeshift morgues made from white dome tents and refrigerated trucks appeared outside of several hospitals in preparation for the dead. There were food and toiletry shortages. Globally, every individual everywhere had to evaluate what was really important—lining up with the world or the Word of God!

What's important to you? How has COVID-19 affected your ability to turn your page(s)? I am not implying God sent these viruses (COVID-19 was manufactured in a lab by man, *not* God) and want to make it clear that I am very empathetic to those who have suffered through it and witnessed loved ones dying from this terrible global pandemic. I believe it caused many in the world to reexamine their priorities and turn toward Jesus instead of away from Him. When world systems fail, like they often do, we have a loving Savior who never fails us. Is this the last virus or plague humans will endure? I doubt it.

> *And Jesus . . . said unto them, take heed that no man deceives you . . . and ye shall hear of wars and rumors of wars: see that ye be not troubled: for all these things must come to pass, but the end is not yet. For nation shall rise against nation, and kingdom against kingdom: and there shall be famines, and* **pestilences***, and earthquakes, in diverse places. All these are the beginning of sorrows. Then shall they deliver you up to be afflicted and shall kill you: and ye shall be hated of all nations for my name's sake. And then shall many be offended, and shall betray one another, and shall hate one another.* **(Matt. 24:5–10)**

The Page We Refuse to Turn

Our choices, or lack of, will also affect others and, depending on our circle, it can be a small or large group of people. The 2020 United States presidential election is a prime example of someone not willing to turn the page and many suffered the consequences of one person's choice. The American people voted, and clearly Joseph Biden was the winner. President Donald Trump refused to concede. His refusal to accept the truth did not change the results. He challenged various states, but the findings were consistent—he lost. Trump tried to convince the American people that there was voter fraud, and the election was stolen, so he believed the election should be overturned.

This assumption caused many Trump supporters to attack the Capitol Building in Washington, DC on January 6, 2021. They sought to disrupt the joint session of Congress assembled to count electoral votes that would formalize President-elect Joe Biden's victory. All news stations, social media, and anyone in the area with a cell phone showed footage of the Capitol complex that had to go on lockdown. Lawmakers and staff were evacuated while supporters-turned-rioters assaulted law enforcement officers and vandalized the building for several hours. There were unnecessary deaths and injuries because *one person* refused to turn their page.

Messed-Up People

Dr. Tony Evans, one of my favorite writers and speakers, wrote in his book *The Kingdom Agenda* (Evans, 2013) about a solution to fixing the culture by starting with your own spheres of influence. We need to reconsider our own lives, our relationship with Christ (or lack of), how we are loving and nurturing our families, and how we serve in our local churches. We live in a fallen world that has lost its morals and its standards while our government is falling apart. Crime continues to rise, children are being trafficked, and illegal drugs are infecting our families; meanwhile, we're just meeting together inside of a building we call church rather than *being* the church.

That's not working for us. There are too many people bringing worldly practices and ideas inside the church instead of taking God's truth into their neighborhoods. We have too many closet Christians who participate in traditional sins just to be accepted and in style—and try to convince themselves and others that it's all right. Everybody else is coming out; Christians might as well come out, too. We tend to think that it is easy to live around sin and somehow not be affected by it. Dr. Evans begged to differ:

> *Because the fact is if you're a messed-up person and you have a family, you are going to contribute to a messed-up family, and if your family goes to church, then your messed-up family will contribute to a messed-up church. And if you're a messed-up person contributing to a messed-up family contributing to a messed-up church, and your church is in a neighborhood, then your messed-up church will lead to a messed-up neighborhood. And if you're a messed-up person contributing to a messed-up family contributing to a messed-up church leading to a messed-up neighborhood, and your neighborhood resides in a city, then your messed-up neighborhood will result in a messed-up city. Now if you're a messed-up person contributing to a messed-up family contributing to a messed-up church leading to a messed-up neighborhood resulting in a messed-up city, and your city resides in a county, then your messed-up city will cause a messed-up county.*
>
> *And if you're a messed-up person contributing to a messed-up family contributing to a messed-up church leading to a messed-up neighborhood resulting in a messed-up city residing in a messed-up county, and your county is part of a state, then your county will help create*

a messed-up state. But that's not all. If you're a messed-up person contributing to a messed-up family contributing to a messed-up church leading to a messed-up neighborhood resulting in a messed-up city residing in a messed-up county helping to create a messed-up state, and your state is part of a country, then your messed-up state helps produce a messed-up nation. Now if you're a messed-up person contributing to a messed-up family contributing to a messed-up church leading to a messed-up neighborhood resulting in a messed-up city helping to create a messed-up state that helps produce a messed-up nation, and your nation is part of the world, your messed-up country will leave us with a messed-up world!

So, if we want a better world composed of better countries, inhabited by better states, made up of better counties, composed of better cities, inhabited by better neighborhoods, illuminated by better churches, made up of better families, we need to become better people. It all starts with personal responsibility—living all of life under God." (Evans, 2013, pg. 524)

Beloved, change starts with *you!* Let Jesus be your security. Want to make a difference? Turn your page(s)! Sometimes our past is so distorted it has taken us into a tangled web we never wanted to enter, so we are not sure how to get unraveled. We must start by learning to fight spiritual warfare on our knees as we pray to the Lord for divine protection, guidance, and strategy to defeat the enemy of our souls. What is spiritual warfare? It is basically the battle between Christians and the forces of darkness or Satan. The three dimensions of spiritual warfare are:

1. The world that we live in and see with our natural eyes
2. The flesh or bodies
3. The Devil

Why is it necessary? The Devil wants to kill, steal, and destroy you and take away your spiritual freedom by keeping you bound in chains of deception (**John 10:10**). If you are bound, you are ineffective to him and his kingdom of darkness. An informed Christian who knows who they are in Christ is his biggest threat. With the full armor of God (**Eph. 6**), you are equipped and liberated to destroy the enemy's camp!

Our children and grandchildren's souls are at stake. We must allow the Holy Spirit to infiltrate our hearts and lives so we can be the godly influence in the hearts and lives of our families, neighbors, and coworkers.

Chapter 4:

What Happens When We Defy Nature?

Why does man want to send astronauts to the moon? Why do people risk their lives to climb Mount Everest year after year? Why are humans fascinated with discovery, exploration, and adventure? Why do we seek praises from other like-minded people, instead of God, through some form of technology to validate our daily quests?

As kids, we watched animated cartoons of superheroes that had us fantasizing about flying or having some superpower that made us impressively dominant over our enemies. I remember putting on goggles and tying a small blanket or towel around my neck as a cape and pretended to fly off of my bed, furniture, or steps of the stairs. Yep, those were different days filled with imagination. As a society, we now have upgraded to movies depicting humans (with the aid of special effects) that possess these extraordinary capabilities and skills like *Black Panther, Wonder Woman, Black Widow, Shang-Chi, Iron Man, Spiderman, The Avengers*, and the list goes on and on. Man's quest to go beyond his nature expresses his character, temperament, and need to control his environment. Why do we want to do this?

It is true, according to **Genesis 1:26–28**, that God gave man "... *dominion over the fish of the sea, and over the fowl of the air, and over the cattle, and over all the earth, and over every creeping thing that creeps upon the earth. And God blessed them, and God said unto them, be* *fruitful, and multiply, and replenish the earth, and subdue it: and have dominion . . . every living thing that moves upon the earth."* Despite this authorization from the Lord, man still tries to challenge these boundaries. Just like in chapter 2 of Genesis, which recounts the story when God placed Adam and Eve in the Garden of Eden with trees of fruits they may eat but forbade them to eat from *"the Tree of the Knowledge of Good and Evil."* They were able to walk and talk with God *every* day, yet somehow, from the many trees of fruit to choose from, they still managed to do what they were commanded *not* to do. What would have happened if Adam and Eve went against their natural desires and never disobeyed God? I submit to you that the world may very well be in a totally different condition if they had never defied God's command.

God established the laws of nature from long-term observation of repeatable patterns and trends to keep order. Meanwhile, the laws of man may vary from culture to culture, based on moral values that fluctuate. For example, in some countries, the death penalty is repulsive, and in others it is embraced. People try to excel in some areas, thinking they can outrun their pasts. They stay stuck in shackles of guilt, shame, humiliation, and degradation. If they can somehow overachieve and control their environment, they can try to pretend the past never happened—only to realize the past does not exactly go away with present day accolades.

They have refused to face their not-so-easily-forgotten former years. Many bank on pushing their thoughts and emotions from the past down deep inside of them, hoping these wrought feelings will never surface; hence, they continue to refuse to turn the page(s) that keep them bound. Sometimes they know it and sometimes they don't. Sometimes man will try to prove that they do not need God to help them deal with their pasts or future. Rebellion and ignorance are not bliss. Instead, it is a never-ending trip inside an endless hole that the enemy uses to keep us constrained in a cycle of captivity. The enemy uses this divisive cycle to keep separation between humans and their loving Creator. Counseling without the Bible is man trying to justify his inexcusable behaviors. Stay connected to the Lord, my friend. When we try to defy nature, we go against God's divine order.

Beloved, stop falling for the enemy's deceptive devices. God created the world, so we need to go to Him for the answers. If your computer breaks down and you can't get it to work properly, you call the company that manufactured or designed the computer to get technical support. Why don't we call on God to help us with everything going on inside our natural bodies and minds? Our world tells us that we can do whatever we put our minds to do and then tries to push further in an attempt to go against God and our natural order of harmony and stability.

So, where do we go when we run out of options and see where our poor choices have taken us? We should start with our Creator. Why? Genesis tells us that God created man and woman. He loved them both. He also made the flesh to cover the spirit while we reside on this side of the grave. The spirit can always overcome the flesh if we exercise discipline. Discipline will only come with practice and walking in righteousness and spiritual authority.

Development, *Not* Punishment

Trust the process that the Lord is doing in and through you. This is all about you seeking Him despite everything going on around you. The Lord loves you unconditionally; He has no desire to hurt or punish you. He desires to see you grow and mature spiritually in leaps and bounds! His actions are to save you from a life of bondage, to develop your spiritual gifts, and see you walk in freedom. He does not send us to hell; we send ourselves by rejecting His Son, Jesus Christ. He has gone way out of His way to ensure we have access to Him through Jesus, who paid the penalty for our sins. His sacrifice is all-encompassing and complete. It cost Him everything. Why would anyone defy or reject Him?

Our only requirement is to simply believe, accept Him as our Lord, and live according to His Word. It costs us nothing to trust Him. We will have to walk away from the sinful crowds and leave unhealthy, wicked lifestyles behind. He desires a loving relationship with all of His children. Get Him off of the shelf and out of the clouds. Read the Bible to understand His character, and cultivate a mutual connection with your heavenly Father. Let Him help you turn the page(s) in your life so you, too, can be liberated from pain and heavy burdens. He is with you, even in your sorrows, *"so do not fear, for I am with you; do not be dismayed, for I am your God. I will strengthen you and help you; I will uphold you with my righteous right hand"* **(Isa. 41:10)**.

Don't get it twisted, we do know that even demons (fallen angels) believe in God. *"You believe that there is one God. Good! Even the demons believe that—and shudder"* **(James 2:19, NIV)**. You must go a step further and accept Jesus into your heart and live and walk in righteousness **(John 3:16; Rom. 10:10)**. Demons are keenly aware of Jesus and His people. **Acts 19:13–14** narrates a story of the seven sons of a Jewish chief priest who were trying to perform an exorcist in the name of the God of the apostle Paul. They would say, *"I bind you by Jesus, whom Paul proclaims. The evil spirit answered and said, Jesus I know, and Paul I know; but who are you?"* How would you respond? The enemy is aware of God's people as outlined in this story, and he acknowledged Jesus and Paul.

Believing is a start, yes, but don't stop there. Salvation is the first step to freedom and turning your page(s) to give you the breakthrough(s) you need to be an overcomer. We live in a fallen world, but as children of God, it is imperative to know and grow into our kingdom heritage. Otherwise, we will be easily tossed to and fro with the enemy's evil strategies. You know what happened to the sons of the Jewish priest who did not have a right relationship with God and tried to help someone get free? *"Then the man (one possessed man) who had the evil spirit jumped on them (there were several) and overpowered them all. He gave them such a beating that they ran out of the house naked and bleeding"* **(Acts 19:16)**.

Unfortunately, that is the fate of many people who refuse to turn their page(s). They are stuck and bound by the enemy who wreaks havoc. He can only do this because people do not know who they are in Christ. Beloved, do you realize that greater is He that is in you than he that is in the world **(1 John 4:4)**?

Chapter 5:

Dare to Be Different

So here's what I want you to do, God helping you: Take your everyday, ordinary life—your sleeping, eating, going-to-work, and walking-around life—and place it before God as an offering. Embracing what God does for you is the best thing you can do for him. Don't become so well-adjusted to your culture that you fit into it without even thinking. Instead, fix your attention on God. Readily recognize what he wants from you, and quickly respond to it. Unlike the culture around you, always dragging you down to its level of immaturity, God brings the best out of you, develops well-formed maturity in you." **(Rom. 12:1–2, MSG)**

As a Christian, God's almighty, powerful Spirit is living inside of you to equip you to be a successful overcomer in every area of your life. Do you accept the challenge? Your mission, should you choose to accept it, will require three major steps:

1. Dare to evaluate
2. Dare to submit
3. Dare to expect results

The first step is to dare to evaluate our priorities and current value systems with the Word of God. Does it line up? Are you evaluating people based on the way that they look, the amount of money they earn, their titles, or their racial/cultural background? The very idea that a female who had a child out of wedlock or a young man who was caught stealing food to feed his siblings could cause many to harshly judge them. The evaluation process starts in your mind. You need to capture your thoughts and not allow them to plant seeds in your heart. If a bad thought or idea starts in our mind and goes unchecked, it will make its way to your heart, and you will begin to speak it.

How can we be so sure of that? The Bible tells us that *"from the abundance of the heart, the mouth speaks"* (**Matt. 12:24**). Beloved, protect your heart and mind so you don't speak negativity and words of death to yourself or make harmful deposits into anyone else who may hear you. Don't give a voice to worldly ideology. Instead, affirmatively declare God's Word. Be different. Speak life to the volume of the book that is written of you to avoid sinful snares.

Second, do you dare to submit yourselves totally to the Lord? Submission means to humble yourself, be vulnerable, and trust God. This is challenging in a world that promotes selfish ambitions (i.e., the "me movement"). In other words, you must realize that it is *not* all about you. You have to get into the attitude that *"He must increase, but I must decrease"* (**John 3:30**). Humility is essential to allowing and believing the process. Vulnerability is giving Him all of your heart, being fully committed, as in there's no turning back. You cannot have one foot in the world and one foot in heaven—that position does not exist! Your heart and intentions will be revealed in the light. You must be willing to be transparent by giving Him all of your fears, problems, and anxieties with full confidence that He will handle your business with care and sensitivity.

You must take God at His Word and believe He means what He says. *"He knows the plans He has for you; plans to prosper you and not to harm you, plans to give you a hope and a future"* (**Jer. 29:11**). My friend, His plans are always for your good and His glory. Your vulnerability is essential to permitting a loving God to release you from vile shackles and empower you to turn the page(s) you desperately try to keep hidden. The world tries to be hard and independent, which only leads to isolation and separation from the Lord. Just look at Facebook and Twitter, filled with so many lonely people looking for affirmation and validation. Dare to stand for righteousness and encourage others to do the same. Sometimes you may be the only light God uses to spread the good news of the gospel. You may be the only Bible some may ever read or listen to, so dare to choose your words wisely. Sometimes others will simply watch your actions and daily living from afar. What do your lifestyle selections say about you?

Once you dare to evaluate according to His Word and dare to submit yourself totally to the Lord, you can dare to expect results. Humans have a way of shaping their expectations that can easily influence their results. We must own it and realize the responsibility is on us, or we can become anxious, upset, even angry, if our perceived expectations crash, fall short, or fail to come to fruition. You can always expect His unconditional, unchanging love for His people. *"For I am convinced that neither death nor life, neither angels nor demons, neither the present nor the future, nor any powers, neither height nor depth, nor anything else in all creation, will be able to separate us from the love of God that is in Christ Jesus our Lord"* **(Rom. 8:38–39)**. You can have the utmost assurance that His eternal, encompassing presence is forever with you no matter what happens. *"And surely I am with you always, to the very end of the age"* **(Matt. 28:20)**. He will never leave you nor forsake you, so trust Him to be with you to face your bondage and turn your page(s). Adjust your faith upward, not downward, so you can expect maximum results.

Unfortunately, most Christians experience just a small portion of what God has provided for His children. **Revelation 4:1–2** tells us to *"come up to a higher perspective."* This means we must seek the Holy Spirit to see things outside of our natural eyes and try God's view. Don't just settle for "same-old, same-old" or nibble at His table or settle for mere table scraps. Beloved, God loves you and has spread a banquet table of blessings for you (**Ps. 23:5**). As a child of the Most High, you are entitled to so much more in greater abundance. God has promised healing, open dialogue with Him, and supernatural experiences to those who love and serve Him (**Eph. 3:14–21**).

So, expect to be blessed by God in these things and more. Jesus says we would do greater things than He did because He would go to the Father (**John 14:12**). Take the limits of God. Dare to be ready and willing to let Him use you beyond what your finite mind can comprehend. You have been lied to for so long that you failed to become who you were created to be. Dare to pray every day with such genuine humility and reverence like the prophet Isaiah and declare, "Here am I, Lord; send me!"

Gatekeepers

The world splashes images of scarcely dressed individuals that cause many to lust after the flesh. As men and women of God, we must dare to be different or risk falling prey to these worldly practices. Instead, we must be careful to filter what we allow inside our gates—what we listen to, watch, see, taste, eat, and touch. My friend, you must also protect the gateway to your sensual and sexual desires. You are responsible for your body and its gates. *"Know ye not that you are the temple of God, and that the Spirit of God dwelleth in you?"* (**1 Cor. 3:16**).

What goes in these gates will plant seeds, good or bad, in our minds, bodies, and souls. Ultimately, what you allow in is what will come out. Choose wisely. Most spouses don't set out to cheat, but they are slowly seduced by images, smells, and entertaining thoughts and ideas that should have been cast down and rejected. Eventually, they give in to what they ponder. People of God, I dare you to turn the filthy, lustful television programs and movies off that portray licentious adults practicing immoral conduct and activities. I dare you to stop giving your money to sinful internet, cable companies, and networks that promote porn and lewd communication.

Gatekeepers tend to deal with things that happen in our lives that have the potential to keep you stuck—they cut you open, but don't tell you what to do to heal! You may have endured starvation, exposure, exploitation, and harassment. You may have dabbled into more worldly or fleshly pleasure than you wanted in order to deaden the pain. Everything can change in one moment (**2 Cor. 1:20**). One bad choice can alter your destiny. Getting into a car with friends who have been drinking can end in tragedy. Saying yes to premarital sex can result in unwanted pregnancy. Acceptance of immorality can spark an unnecessary dependence on drugs and alcohol while laying a foundation of abuse for the next generation. Protecting your gates is essential to growth.

Think of it like an actual gatekeeper in the Old Testament of the Bible, who was appointed and chosen by the king. This person had the daily responsibility to protect the temple and keep the city safe (**2 Kings 7:10–11**). This person had to be devoted, consistent, and trustworthy. They were empowered to determine who could and could not enter. Equally, God requires us to be gatekeepers in the spiritual realm. Beloved, be different. Protect your temple so you can guard your family, home, and church. God desires that you be a gatekeeper in all domains of your life (**Prov. 8:34–35**).

What are you allowing into your gates? If you continue to do what the world does, you will get the same results they do and end up in hell. *"Enter through the narrow gate; for the gate is wide and the way is broad that leads to destruction, and there are many who enter through it"* (**Matt. 7:13, NASB**). Letting anything in your gates is what keeps you bound to a biased, confused world system orchestrated by the enemy. Dare to swipe off the dust of your past as you let the Lord help you turn your page(s) that seek to destroy you. Dare to be an unshakable and faithful gatekeeper.

Chapter 6:
No Manufacturer's Recall

When a person "turns" their page(s), Merriam-Webster.com states that it means to change in position or to change course or direction. So, when we refuse to turn the page(s), there is no forward motion. Without that redirect progress, we are essentially in the enemy's holding pattern that deems us ineffective, inadequate, and unsuccessful in that area. However, a product "recall" is a request from a manufacturer to return a product after the discovery of safety issues or product defects that might endanger the consumer or put the maker/seller at risk of legal action. God knew you before you were formed in your mother's womb (**Jer. 1:5; Ps. 139:13–16**). He is *not* the author of confusion (**1 Cor. 14:33**), nor was He ever baffled about who He created you to be.

Every life matters. *Your life matters.* You have great purpose in His kingdom. God can use any willing vessel.

Due to your reluctance to turn the page(s), God has found some defects in your heart, eyes, and feet. The Lord wants to use Jesus to help you recall these issues to avoid danger, security, or protection issues of your soul. Let's start with the heart. We don't love like we ought or used to; instead, we hold back to prevent what we see as potential or further pain. There was a time you loved everyone with your whole heart, until it got broken. Someone intentionally or unintentionally hurt you. Inadvertently, you stopped loving, thinking you were shielding or guarding your own heart; however, in reality you could've given your shattered pieces to the Lord to mend and make you better, not bitter.

Beloved, **Hebrews 12:15 (NLT)** tells us to *"look after each other so that none of you fails to receive the grace of God. Watch out that no poisonous root of bitterness grows up to trouble you, corrupting many."* Your actions, or lack thereof, affect other people, so we *must* begin with ourselves. We *must* end the vicious sequence of hurting others or meeting sin on the same level to one-up the other person(s). Vengeance belongs to the Lord **(Rom. 12:19)**. Above all, please remember to love each other deeply, for love covers a multitude of sins **(1 Pet. 4:8)**. Your breakthrough comes through love, not hate or sin. For out of the abundance of the heart, the mouth speaks **(Luke 6:45)**, so try to keep pure things in you so that's what will come out. Fill your heart with His love and His Word to escape unnecessary spiritual recall(s).

Second, you have allowed your natural eyes to supersede your spiritual eyes. How? You have been so distracted and focused on the circumstances of life that you don't see anything God's way. Please understand that since God is higher, He can see further. Bad things can happen to godly people and good things can happen to bad people. There are some people who feel let down by God, and they get angry and confused; then sadly, some will walk away from the faith. It usually starts out that a person will continuously ask God to do something—like heal their grandmother—and He does not do it. They got angry and concluded that since they cannot see God anyway, He must not exist. **John 11** describes a righteous man named Lazarus who was sick, and Jesus loved him. Even after He received the word about Lazarus being ill, He stayed two days longer—not rushing to see his sick friend. He was not making any moves toward him, but He continued to speak.

Do you trust God's Word *before* you see any manifestation? If God speaks it, get ready because it's happening! Learn to trust God's Word before you see His intervention. **Second Kings 6:17** tells us that the prophet Elisha told his servant to not be afraid because those who are with them are more than those who are not. He prayed, *"O Lord,* *open his eyes so he may see."* Then the Lord opened the servant's eyes, and he looked and saw the hills full of horses and chariots of fire all around Elisha.

Beloved, do not allow the cares of this world to take your focus off of our loving Savior. His plans are always for our best. Ask the Lord to open your spiritual eyes to see things His way and not allow anything to distract you. His answers are not always what you may want; however, from His vantage point, He knows what He is doing and how it all fits together. That statement can hit hard and deep since most people want their way. Still, I encourage you to have faith in the one who can see it all to help you turn the page(s).

Third, your feet are in a rebellion that is taking you in totally different directions away from the Lord. There was a time when you prayed and listened for God's direction before you made any moves. Sadly now, you pursue money and materialism so you can feel like you have made it. Nobody wants to see you blessed more than God, but this chase of mammon only ends in emptiness. We get impatient when we only see or feel what is in front of us, so we allow the influence of the world to set our priorities for us. The world says the material things we can see and touch should take precedence in our lives, but there is no peace or fulfillment in these objects. I am not against having things, but they should never be your god or take His place in your heart. Seek God's guidance on everything and remember to follow through with whatever He tells you. God will do His part, but we must do ours.

Using the Lazarus example in the previous paragraph **(John 11)**, once Jesus arrived back to Bethany at Mary and Martha's village (Lazarus's sisters), their brother had already died. Jesus was well aware of this and timed it perfectly. He asked them to remove the stone that covered the tomb of Lazarus. Could Jesus have commanded the stone to move on His own with His words? Of course, but He told the people around the tomb to do it. Once they did their part, Jesus called Lazarus *by name* to come forth out of the grave. Think about it. He could've hurried back and healed Lazarus so he would not have died; however, He allowed this situation, brought him back from the grave where a whole revival broke out in the village, and many were saved! Clearly, His plan was bigger and better! **Proverbs 3:5–6** tells us to *"trust in the Lord with all thy heart and lean not upon thine own understanding. In all thy ways acknowledge him, and he will direct thy paths,"* and show you how and where to go to turn your page(s) without the need for a recall.

The ultimate recall is found in **Jeremiah 18:1–6** when God is talking to His prophet about His ability to work with any willing vessel since He is the Potter; however, verse 6 tells us that His people are not adaptable. As the Potter, He controls the wheel that turns the vessel as He delicately uses His hands to make and mold the clay into a beautiful piece of sculpture. The wheel is necessary but not always welcomed by the clay or vessel. The wheel is circumstances of life used through trials and tribulations we endure to make us pliable. To murmur and complain against your circumstances is to groan against God. The clay has to be flexible and freely submitted to the Potter to smooth out the rough, lumpy edges.

As God's people, we stay stuck on disbelief and the many distractions of our temporary situations. We get caught griping to our friends and forget about seeking the Potter. The substance of clay is plenteous and found everywhere, so realize everyone will have an opinion, but only God's opinion matters. A real friend will direct you to God, and not entertain the foolishness or allow you to stay there. Beloved, please remember that one touch from the Potter can transform your life. Are you ready to turn the page(s) in your life? Fully submit to the Potter and let Him change you into a beautiful vessel.

Deeper Walk or Plow Pusher?

Favor takes a deeper level of faith. How? Favor with the Lord will get you jobs you are not qualified for in the natural. The Lord will open a door to get you in, and you must depend on Jesus to equip you, not ahead of time, but as you go. Those He sends, He equips. Likewise, God knows exactly where you need to be and who you need to be with in order to fulfill your life assignment. He is always working everything out for our good (**Rom. 8:28**). As He did in the life of Paul, God will use every aspect of who you are and where you came from to bring about His will in your life. He is not distracted by your background, your level of education, your past occupations, or everything else you've accumulated from your life experiences. He can use everything and create opportunities to lead you into places where you are surrounded by unfamiliar faces to teach you lessons that you couldn't learn any other way. One thing is certain: If God has called you, He will equip you for the task; just be willing and dependent on Him. You can take that to the bank and cash it every time!

Plow pushers work hard, constantly looking to make that next dollar at all costs. Look out, I may be coming to your house now. Sometimes we have to give up plan B and *only* pursue plan A. What does this mean? Let go of the backup plans we think we need in order to make it in life. God may be showing you that He wants to prosper you in plan A, but we keep dividing our time and attention on plan B—you know, our side hustles, our backup wife/girlfriends or husband/boyfriends, and so on. We never really go because we are never fully committed to anything or anyone, especially not God. Let go of the nonsense and do *only* what God has for *you*.

Favor will not make a lot of sense, but it will propel you where you need to go at the appointed time. Have a made-up mind to completely pursue the Lord and hold on for many adventures! The journey is worth every step as He woos you and showers you with His blessings to turn pages in your life and help others do the same just by your lifestyle. You will be challenged, but He is with you every step of the way. Have an open heart and willing ear to follow the leading of the Holy Spirit. God will guide you and prepare the path ahead of you. Therefore, trust Him to complete the work He has begun in you for every phase of your life.

Chapter 7:

Transformation

Beloved, we have learned throughout these pages about the consequences of being stuck, whether we are aware of it or not, and how the lack of movement and painful experiences has caused us to view life through filters of sorrow, heartache, and anguish as we refuse to turn the page(s) of our lives. We have become uncomfortably comfortable with being broken and thirsty. Some are desperately seeking to manage their expectations as they seek help through the medical professionals or mask their pain in substance and alcohol addiction.

We examined how to stretch beyond our emotional bondages and where to go for stability and strength. We learned that for us to walk in freedom, we must implement forgiveness as a way of life. Being an undercover Christian is to believe in false evidence appearing real. Reading God's truth in the Bible is essential to growing and maturing in a relationship with Him. We examined the truth of not having to walk in fear, but to receive and embrace His unconditional love. We were made aware that if we continue to stay stuck, our choices will affect everyone around us. Pestilences and natural disasters will happen, but God is always in control. We learned that as Christians, we need to come out of the closet and be the church because those four walls are just a building. We know that going against nature is to go against God's divine order.

Additionally, we explored the concept of our loving, heavenly Father wanting to develop us, *not* punish us. We learned that if we accept the challenge to be different, everything can change in one moment—for good or bad depending on our choices. Being a wise gatekeeper will take you in the right direction. We learned that the Great Creator did not make any mistakes, but our unwillingness to turn our page(s) has Him wanting to recall the things out of our lives that have us bound.

Think of it like this. Unresolved issues are like wet cement that will harden overnight. It gets more challenging to get rid of once it settles. There is no time limit on negative emotions, so don't give a foothold to the enemy. Thriving relationships with yesterday's baggage will not survive. All of this luggage gets rehearsed and rehashed over and over in the mind. We must begin a transformational life by transforming our minds or thinking patterns. Chapter 5 discussed taking your thoughts captive, so we do not allow it to fester and move into our hearts.

How do we transform our minds? Start by building up your faith. Remember, faith is the process, not the end result. Salvation, not just believing there is a God, is outlined in the next steps:

1. Admitting you are a sinner in need of God 's grace starts you on the right path
2. Believing that Jesus died on the cross for your sins
3. Confessing your sins to a loving God and accepting Jesus as your Lord and Savior

These are very personal steps to changing your life forever. Going from an edgy, toughened criminal to a respectable, stable man or woman of God after an amazing encounter with our loving Savior is the biggest miracle anyone can experience. You have *everything* to gain and *nothing* to lose. Start reading the Bible to feast on decency, decorum, and dignity for your soul and spirit to help you turn the page(s) of your life.

As you accept Jesus as your Lord and begin to feed your mind righteousness, you can expect transformational living. One revelation from the Lord can reframe your entire life. The Bible is filled with rich history and prophecy. One disclosure of a golden nugget can change the whole trajectory of a person's life. Saul of Tarsus was temporarily blinded by the Lord for three days after Jesus revealed Himself to him **(Acts 9:1-19)**. Up to that point, Saul used to hunt Christians and kill them. His life was so wreaked and rearranged by the revelation of Christ that Saul became the apostle Paul and took the gospel to the Gentiles. Like many of us, Paul had moments where he felt the challenges of everyday living, even when he was in prison, but he did not faint in doing good.

Sometimes, you will not have the convenience of someone supporting or inspiring you with wisdom when things happen that don't seem to be fair. When you are stressed and feel afflicted, like King David when his people spoke of stoning him, you have to learn to stir up that spirit within you and *"encourage yourself in the Lord your God"* **(1 Sam. 30:6)**. Do not depend on others for something that Christ can do within you. Sometimes, especially in the middle of the night or in the middle of a storm when only the Holy Spirit is available, you will have to recollect His promises and assurances that you read in the Bible. You may have to speak to your storm and tell it about your God. Let this mind that is in Christ Jesus be in *you* **(Phil. 2:5)**.

Don't praise God for the horrible storm; tell the storm that you are a King's kid and that it has no rights to you! Tell the enemy to take his hands off of you, your marriage, and your family! Speak the appropriate scripture(s) to your situation. Holy boldness and transformational living only come through prayer (communication with your heavenly Father), fasting (denial of food and spending that time in prayer), and reading or feasting on the Word of God to get the strength you need to turn the page(s) of your life. You will never know what it means to live a transformed life if you are not willing to give your best. As discussed in chapter 2, God gave His best, His *only* Son, who willingly sacrificed Himself for you. Your freedom cost Him everything. **Matthew 6:21** states, *"for where your treasure is, there your heart will be also."*

What do you do with the things you value most? I know you work hard at your job and try to stretch your dollars every month. Trust me, the money you give or hold back from God's kingdom will not break Him or any concept of a bank in heaven. He doesn't need your money; it's your heart He desires. When you give, *"it will be given back to you good measure, pressed down, and shaken together, and running over, shall men give into your bosom. For with the same measure that ye mete withal it shall be measured to you again"* (**Luke 6:38**). The Message puts it this way: *"Give away your life; you'll find life given back, but not merely given back—given back with bonus and blessing. Giving, not getting, is the way. Generosity begets generosity."*

Always offer your best with finances, talents, skills, and volunteer time. The Lord is the one who gives you gifts and abilities that are irrevocable (**Rom. 11:29**); what you do with them is up you. We all have to balance our lives with the same twenty-four hours, but our resources may be very different based on our choices with our talents, skills, and gifts. No matter your plight, your volunteer hours can be used to make a difference in a child's life as a little league coach or hosting children's Bible study in your house or virtually. Do you cook? Do you crochet/knit socks or blankets? There are many cancer patients who could use a warm meal or covering during chemotherapy, not to mention homeless people who would appreciate the nourishment and clean socks. You really can make a conscious choice to generate blessings that create differences in the lives of others in your community where you are right now. Get active; get involved. See how the Lord will move on your behalf to help you move forward to change the page(s) of your life and use you to support others through your example.

Keep in mind that finances are one area in the Bible that the Lord asks His people to "test" Him. **Malachi 3:10** states, *"Bring the whole tithe into the storehouse, that there may be food in my house. Test me in this, says the LORD Almighty, and see if I will not throw open the floodgates of heaven and pour out so much blessing that you will not have room enough for it."* Beloved, put God to the test to be a recipient of His faithfulness.

If you give little, you get little. If you give generously, you receive generously. If you want a transformational life, walk in generosity, and always give your absolute best—not leftovers or something that you no longer want. You cannot give haphazardly and expect to yield a big harvest. Dear saints, please be aware that you can never outgive God!

When your life is transformed by receiving His salvation, reading His Word to start thinking and living a transformational existence, it will lead to the full manifestation of transformation as a lifestyle so you will soar like an eagle—leaving behind your will and inability to turn page(s) in your life. This is more than a nice theory; the manifestation or appearance, expression, or demonstration of an exciting, get-up-and-go life so converted, changed, and altered by the Lord does not come overnight. It takes discipline and restraint to understand and walk in your God-given authority. Train for an imperishable crown so you have something to lay before Jesus (**1 Cor. 9:25**).

You need to be in constant communication with the Holy Spirit and believing with your whole heart that you are who the Lord says you are in the Bible! He has empowered you to become fruitful as you put on the full armor of God since you do not wrestle against flesh and blood, but against principalities, powers, the rulers of the darkness of this age, and spiritual hosts of wickedness in the heavenly places (**Eph. 6:12**). Be careful not to allow the worries of this life, the deceitfulness of wealth, and the desire for other things come in and choke the Word so that it becomes unfruitful (**Mark 4:19**). If you continue in the faith and not grow weary, you can utter a simple prayer without doubt, and expect it to be executed and fulfilled.

Adversity bring opportunity—it's all a matter of perspective and whose report you choose to believe. Show love in action and be the light the world needs now before it is too late. Watch your life transform so the Lord can set you free from everything that keeps you bound and tries to stop you from turning the page(s) of your life. As a Christian, you are not alone and believe me when I say that the body of Christ loves you and is pulling for you every step of the way. The world needs your voice, your talents, and your skills. The Lord desires *you* to be whole. Your life makes a difference. If you are still here on this side of the grave, then you have more work to do and people to reach with the good news of the gospel. With the help of Christ, get delivered by turning the page(s) of your book right now!

Notes

Evans, Tony (2013). *The Kingdom Agenda* (p. 524). Moody Publishers. Kindle Edition.

Gillespie, Claire. How Are the Spanish Flu and COVID-19 Alike? Here's What Doctors Say. (17 November 2020) https://www.health.com/condition/infectious-diseases/how-are-spanish-flu-and-covid-19-alike

Peterson, Eugene (2000). *A Long Obedience in the Same Direction*, 2nd Edition. IVP Publishers. p. 16.

(All Bible verses used throughout the book are King James Version unless otherwise stated).

CPSIA information can be obtained
at www.ICGtesting.com
Printed in the USA
BVHW041418140223
658283BV00041B/652